Grandpa's Basement

Corinne M. Litzenberg
Illustrations by Bari A. Edwards

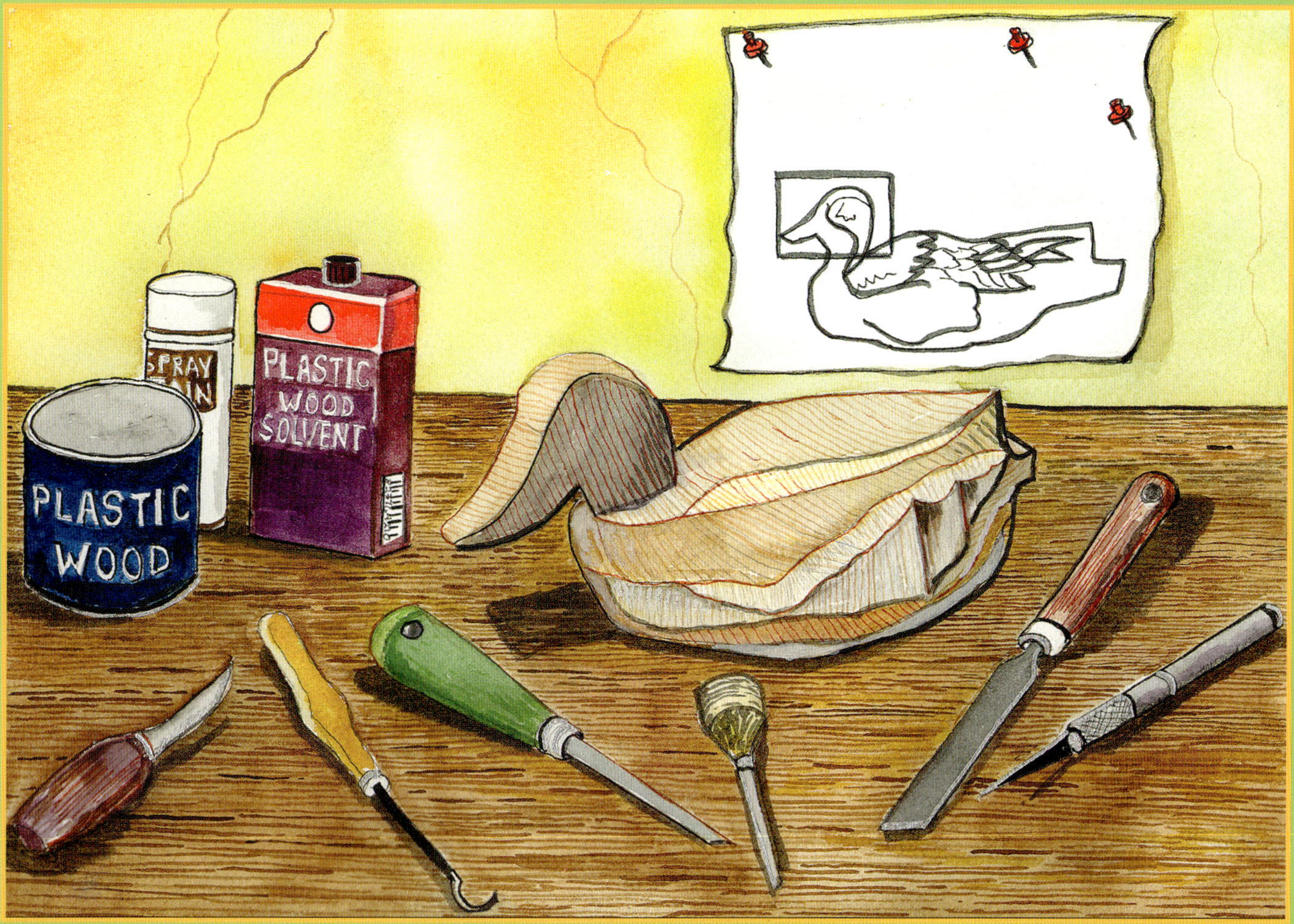

4880 Lower Valley Road, Atglen, Pennsylvania 19310

Other Schiffer Books by Corinne M. Litzenberg
The Sand Lady: A Cape May Tale
The Sand Lady: An Ocean City Maryland Tale

Other Schiffer Books on Related Subjects
The Art of the Decoy: American Bird Carvings. Adele Earnest
Contemporary Bird Carvings: Two Generations of Bird Carvers. Kenneth Basile
Decoys of the Mid-Atlantic Region. Henry A. Fleckenstein
The Making of Hunting Decoys. William Veasey
Upper Chesapeake Bay Decoys and Their Makers. David & Joan Hagan
Wading & Shore Birds of the Atlantic Coast. Roger S. Everett

Copyright © 2007 by Corinne M. Litzenberg
Library of Congress Control Number: 2007925040

All rights reserved. No part of this work may be reproduced or used in any form or by any means—graphic, electronic, or mechanical, including photocopying or information storage and retrieval systems—without written permission from the publisher.

The scanning, uploading and distribution of this book or any part thereof via the Internet or via any other means without the permission of the publisher is illegal and punishable by law. Please purchase only authorized editions and do not participate in or encourage the electronic piracy of copyrighted materials.

"Schiffer," "Schiffer Publishing Ltd. & Design," and the "Design of pen and ink well" are registered trademarks of Schiffer Publishing Ltd.

Designed by "Sue"
Type set in BankGothic Md BT/Humanist 521 BT
ISBN: 978-0-7643-2720-9
Printed in China

Published by Schiffer Publishing Ltd.
4880 Lower Valley Road
Atglen, PA 19310
Phone: (610) 593-1777; Fax: (610) 593-2002
E-mail: Info@schifferbooks.com

For the largest selection of fine reference books on this and related subjects, please visit our web site at www.schifferbooks.com
We are always looking for people to write books on new and related subjects. If you have an idea for a book please contact us at the above address.

This book may be purchased from the publisher.
Include $3.95 for shipping.
Please try your bookstore first.
You may write for a free catalog.

In Europe, Schiffer books are distributed by
Bushwood Books
6 Marksbury Ave.
Kew Gardens
Surrey TW9 4JF England
Phone: 44 (0) 20 8392-8585; Fax: 44 (0) 20 8392-9876
E-mail: info@bushwoodbooks.co.uk
Website: www.bushwoodbooks.co.uk
Free postage in the U.K., Europe; air mail at cost.

Dedication

For my uncles, Robert B. Petro and G. Edward Petro

In memory of my father, Leonard Weiss, and my brothers, Jeff and Drew

To Dr. K, to read with your grandchildren, with appreciation as a great doctor who has saved many lives!

Corinne M. Fitzenberg
9.95.2020

Bobby knelt next to the glass-topped coffee table, playing a game of checkers with his Grandma.

"Your turn, Grandma," he said.

Grandma sat in her favorite spot, the soft cushioned, wrought iron chair nearest the porch screen. How she loved to sit for hours watching her birds.

"Just look at those goldfinches feeding upside-down, Bobby!" she exclaimed. "And yesterday we had a pair of mourning doves on the front lawn."

Grandma gazed out the window at her bird paradise, forgetting she was playing checkers with her grandson. Birds and animals of all kinds seem to naturally flock to Bobby's grandparents' backyard year 'round. Even the neighbor's cat, Midnight, chose a corner of their yard to have her litter.

"Grandma... it's your turn. You're red," Bobby reminded her.

Grandma slowly focused back on the game. She moved her checker and Bobby jumped two of her game pieces.

"Oops, looks like you beat me again. That's three games in a row that you've won. You're really getting good at this," Grandma commented.

From the back porch, the buzzing of Grandpa's power saw could be heard. He was cutting down the tall white pine tree that had grown too close to the telephone cables. He sawed the large pieces straight through the heartwood at a firm and steady pace. Then he began to split the thick trunk sections with his axe.

"Watch out for my bluebird box!" Grandma called. "Love my bluebirds!"

She eased out of her chair and reached for her cane. Bobby and his grandmother walked outside to check on him.

Grandpa rested his saw on the ground for a well earned break. A cool breeze blew through the yard, and cherry tree blossoms drifted to the ground like confetti all around Grandpa. Bobby ran under the tree next to him to catch the petal shower. He spun around in circles looking straight up through the tree branches.

Grandpa pulled off his work gloves. Arching his back, he took off his hat and wiped his sweaty forehead with his wrist.

"Rain by evenin'," Grandpa predicted. "Feel it in ma bones. Got anymore of that lemonade, Esther?"

Grandma Esther went to fetch him a nice cold tumbler and Bobby followed her.

"Here Bobby, take this out to your Grandpa and tell him he's done enough work for one day" she said.

She wrapped a dry paper towel around the tumbler and handed it to him with both hands.

As Bobby carried Grandpa's lemonade, he was careful not to trip over any branches or logs lying on the ground.

"What'cha gonna do with all this wood?" Bobby asked.

Grandpa answered, "These pieces gonna make me some nice *decoys*...wooden ducks...like the kind you have at home."

Grandpa gulped down his drink and smacked his lips.

Pointing with the glass in his hand, he continued, "See that piece there...good white pine. It'd make a nice mallard."

Carrying the pitcher of lemonade, Esther interrupted, "Oh no you're not. You know what the doctor said. All that sawdust will clog up your lungs again. No more ducks."

"A few won't take long to hand chop and carve, Esther," Grandpa retorted.

Grandma just shook her head as she refilled his tumbler.

Grandpa rubbed Bobby's head and pressed him close to his side.

"You're gettin' big, son. You're about ready for your first carvin' lesson, too."

Resting his hands on his knees, Grandpa stooped low to speak to Bobby.

"If it's okay with your daddy, we'll start next week when you're off for spring vacation. Sure could use the company. How does that sound?"

Grinning from ear to ear, Bobby shoved his hands deep inside his pants pockets and tried to hold back his excitement. How he had waited to hear Grandpa say those words one day!

"Well," Esther persisted, "tomorrow is another day. Why don't you call it quits? Bobby can help you pile these limbs before the rain comes tonight."

Bobby was eager to help his grandfather pick up the sappy boughs and stack the wood. All he could think about was carving his first duck. He felt certain that his parents would let him. After all, it was spring break and there was no school.

Grandpa praised Bobby, "Good job, son. Now go on in and wash that sap off your hands and say good-bye to your grandmother."

Grandpa hugged Bobby and rubbed his head.

"We'll see ya," he said.

Bobby did as he was told then rode his bike two blocks home. He parked his bike in the garage and lumbered up the back deck steps. His parents were sitting on the deck reading the daily newspaper before dinner.

"Well, how's Grandma and Grandpa?" his father asked as he turned the page of the paper.

"Oh, just fine" Bobby informed them. Then out of the blue he asked, "Dad, can I learn to carve with Grandpa? He said you did when you were about my age."

Bobby's question surprised his father. His mom and dad lowered their newspaper sections and looked at each other.

"Come to think of it, I was about your age, Bobby. If it's okay with your mom, then it's okay with me," his father replied.

Bobby looked over at his mother for her answer. His mother smiled and nodded her head yes.

"That sounds like a great idea to me," she said.

Bobby's face beamed. He rattled on about how there was no school next week and how he helped Grandpa stack the wood. His parents were happy that Bobby had taken such an interest in Grandpa's hobby at such a young age.

That night it stormed, just like Grandpa said it would. Rain pelted the roof and the gutters so hard that Bobby couldn't get to sleep. The rain made him think of ducks, and ducks made him think of carving with Grandpa. He shut his eyes tightly and covered his ears with his pillow. Some time that night, Bobby finally slept.

Spring vacation started on Monday. Bobby rode his bike to his grandparents' house. Ringing his bike bell, he coasted down the same narrow path that led to the back sun porch. He knew he would find his grandmother in her favorite chair. Clutching her bible, she sat listening to her morning Christian radio service. Sunlight beamed through the screen and warmed her arms. She softly tapped her foot on the tile floor to the hymn on the radio.

"Good morning, Grandma. Where's Grandpa?" Bobby asked cheerfully.

"He's in the basement, Bobby…choppin' and sandin' ducks again. Not good for him I tell 'im, but he's been expecting you," she answered.

Bobby leaned his bike against the porch and scurried up the steps. He walked quickly past Grandma and headed straight for the basement door.

"Bobby," Grandma asked, "you let me know if he starts coughin' down there, ya hear?"

Bobby turned to his grandmother respectfully and said, "Yes, Grandma."

Then he took a blueberry muffin from the coffee table for the trip to the basement and gave her a quick hug.

Heading down the stairs he called, "Whatcha doin', Grandpa?"

He took a bite of the moist, crumbly muffin and glanced around the cluttered workshop. Old farm tools and duck patterns hung neatly on nail heads, all in a row. Brushes and gallons of paint lined the shelves. *Audubon* calendar pictures and tattered decoy show posters decorated the walls. On the worktable was a set of ten mallards which Grandpa had just finished hand chopping. Pine shavings were scattered on the floor and sawdust floated through beams of sunlight streaking through the basement windows.

Straddled on his workbench, Grandpa sipped his coffee. His arthritis made him wince.

Grandpa set his hatchet down and rubbed his right wrist, "Hatchet needs a rest...so does my hand. Ahhh, you've got one of Esther's muffins. She makes the best...best coffee, too. I remember when I'd go on my huntin' trips, your Grandma would pack me a big bag of goodies. She'd pack me those same blueberry muffins and fudge brownies, too. Had to watch my bag in the *duck blind* or my buddies would find 'em. She didn't have to make the coffee, though. Nope. Made our own coffee from river water." Grandpa smiled, "Yes sirree."

He was getting that faraway look in his eyes, as if he was living back in those gunnin' days on the river again. Bobby waited patiently for him to continue with his story. His Grandpa liked to tell stories. Some of his tales were long and tall, yet Bobby wanted to believe them all.

"The river was so clear you could drink it if you had to. Why, you could stand hip deep in the river and still see your feet through the water. Sometimes you could see the fish as clear as day right through the water," Grandpa said.

Grandpa pointed to the stuffed *canvasback drake* hanging from the ceiling.

"You see that duck, Bobby. Why, that was the last canvasback shot on the river and I got 'im. I was some duck hunter back in those days. A sure shot."

Bobby knew that he was about to tell one of his stories by the twinkle in his blue eyes and the way he rubbed his gray, bristly whiskers on his chin. Bobby shoved the rest of the muffin in his mouth, leaned against the worktable, and listened to Grandpa.

Grandpa raised his arm and pointed to a batch of decoys he had finished painting.

"And see those decoys. In my day, you could buy 'em for fifty cents a duck. Today, one bird'll go for hundreds at auction."

Grandpa's voice was fading.

He rasped, "Why the sky was black with ducks. We could kill as many as we could carry. Those were the days. Nothin' for them to eat here now. There was so much *wild celery* and grass in the river and the bay, it was hard to motor a boat through. Not anymore. It's like a restaurant, Bobby. If you stop servin' good food, the customers won't come anymore. Nothin' much left here for ducks to feed on. No reason for them to stay."

Grandpa finished his last drop of coffee and set his mug on the table. He gently rubbed his hatchet handle.

"See this hatchet, Bobby? I hand chopped all my ducks with this one… never missed a beat. Carver's gotta have a good, sharp hatchet."

Grandpa showed Bobby his head patterns and decoys. Some were just "roughed out" or hand chopped, while others were painted and needed feather work and eyes.

"Easiest to start with a full-size canvasback," Grandpa instructed. "They're easy to paint and not much feather detail on 'em. All carvers who gunned for a livin' made a 'can' ... it's a good starter duck and best tastin', too."

From that day forward, Bobby spent most of his free time in Grandpa's basement working on his first decoy, a canvasback drake. Every day he learned a basic lesson in carving and listened to his Grandpa's stories. Grandpa hand chopped the body and head for Bobby.

He told his grandson, "Gotta have a good eye. *Symmetry* and balance are important. A good workin' decoy has got to be able to float on the water."

Then Bobby nailed the head on tightly as Grandpa held the duck body.

He taught Bobby how to smoothly sand a bird. When Bobby thought he had his duck as smooth as it could be, he handed it to Grandpa for inspection. Grandpa examined it carefully and circled any rough spots with a pencil that needed more sanding.

"Go with the grain," Grandpa would say as he watched Bobby sand his first duck and blow the sawdust off the pinewood.

Grandpa said, "Go with the grain when you sand. Those little lines in the wood are the grain. They're made when a tree grows. Follow those lines when you sand and you can't go wrong. Yep, Bobby, go with the grain."

Next, Grandpa taught him how to use a carving knife. He showed Bobby how to safely hold the knife and where to place his fingers on the handle. Grandpa carved out one nostril on the duck's bill and Bobby carefully carved out the other.

Finally, Bobby was ready to paint his duck. Grandpa had brushes of every size and oil paints of every duck feather color you could imagine, from bright purples and reds for his *wood duck* drakes to mottled shades of brown and grays for his *hens*.

"Wrap all my brushes separately in newspaper with a little paint thinner. It keeps the bristles nice and neat," Grandpa continued. "For starters, we need to paint this canvasback white for a base coat. All decoys need at least one good base coat," he told Bobby.

Grandpa said, "A base coat is an undercoat of white paint on the wood. It acts as a sealer and gives you a clean surface to work on, like a painter's canvas, Bobby. It makes a difference when you start painting with your colors."

Grandpa showed him how to "feather" a bird to make it look like it could fly away. He dipped his fine-tipped brush into the clamshell filled with paint.

"Lift up on your brush with each stroke and he'll start comin' to life," Grandpa instructed.

Bobby watched closely as Grandpa modeled each stroke. Then Grandpa passed the brush to him so he could try. Bobby's tongue held tightly on the corner of his mouth as he firmly gripped his brush and tried to make each feather look just like Grandpa's.

For days, Grandpa and Bobby worked together in the basement. At last, Bobby's first decoy was finished.

"All that's left now is to sign 'im. An artist always signs his work," Grandpa said. "But we'd better wait 'til tomorrow when he's nice and dry."

Every evening over dinner, Bobby told his Mom and Dad how much fun he had had in Grandpa's basement. From start to finish, he told them every detail of the canvasback decoy they had made together, including Grandpa's secret painting tips… like the way he took care of all of his brushes so that they would last a long time.

"And Grandpa showed me how to wrap my paint brushes with just a little paint thinner in newspaper. Then he told me the story about the last canvasback shot on the river and *he's got it!*"

"Oh, he told you *that* one," chuckled his father.

Bobby's mom grinned, "He certainly is a storyteller."

"Yeah," agreed Bobby. " One night, we sat on the porch watching the lightning bugs and listening to the whippoorwills, and Grandpa kept on talking. Grandma listened, too. Sometimes she pretends like she never heard his stories before. She laughs, too."

Bobby thought about his decoy again.

"Now all that's left to do is sign my duck. Can I ride my bike over tomorrow?" Bobby asked.

"*May* I ride, " his mother corrected. "Yes, you may, son. Just don't stay too long. After all the hard work you two have done this week, Grandpa's going to need his rest," she reminded him.

Bobby smiled and finished his dinner. Then he helped his dad clear the table while his mom rinsed the dishes and stacked them in the dishwasher. He felt lucky that he could do something special with just his Grandpa and spend time getting to know both of his grandparents a little more.

The next morning, Bobby woke up, anxious to sign his first decoy and bring it home to surprise his parents. He took the familiar route down the tree-lined street to his grandparents' house. Mrs. Gomez, the mail carrier, called to him on the sidewalk from the mail truck.

"Good morning, Bobby," she said. "When you get to your grandparents' house, bring in the mail for them. It'll save you Grandma a trip."

Bobby coasted carefully past Mrs. Gomez and called back to her that he would. He grabbed the mail out of the box with one hand and walked his bike around the back of the house. He called for his Grandma. She was not in her favorite chair watching her birds. Concerned, Bobby quietly entered the kitchen through the back porch, calling softly for both of them. Grandma was in the hallway carrying a bed tray.

"Where's Grandpa?" Bobby asked.

"He's in the bedroom with the nurse."

Grandma bit her lower lip and shook her head.

"All that choppin' and sandin' was too much for him," she added in a trembling voice.

"May I please see him," asked Bobby. "Just for a minute?"

"No, I'm afraid not today, honey. Come back tomorrow. And please have your father call me," she said. "Take that bag of muffins on the counter home with you. No sense in them going to waste."

Grandma tied the plastic grocery bag around Bobby's wrist.

"You'll be able to see him tomorrow," she assured him. "He just needs to rest."

Grandma gave him a tight hug and Bobby kissed her on her soft cheek.

At home, Bobby shared the news with his parents and talked about Grandpa over one of Grandma's muffins and a glass of milk. He understood what his parents told him about Grandpa's health and how he "overdoes it" sometimes working in the basement. He was feeling badly for his Grandpa and wanted to do something special for him.

Bobby walked quietly up to his room and rested on the bed. He decided to made Grandpa a "Get Well" card. On the front he penciled and colored a canvasback drake. On the inside of the card, he wrote a special message:

That evening, Bobby's father called Grandma to check on Grandpa. Since Bobby's father liked to use a speaker phone, Bobby could follow their conversation. Grandma said Grandpa would have to take it easy for a while but he would be up to a visit from Bobby tomorrow. Besides, his duck was finished and it only needed to be signed. It's not like Grandpa would be in basement with all that sawdust again.

Bobby's father asked, "Do you think Dad would be willing to let me put in that new vent system now to keep the sawdust down, Mom?"

Esther replied, "Your father's never been interested in changing that workshop, but this may be your chance, Son. He's stubborn, but I think he may be ready for a little help now, if it'll keep down the dust and let him carve more, especially now that Bobby's learning to carve."

Knowing that his father could help out Grandpa made Bobby feel somehow both reassured and proud.

The next day after breakfast, Bobby tucked his card in his tee-shirt pocket and rambled downstairs for breakfast.

His mother reminded him, "Now don't stay too long."

"Don't worry, I won't," he replied.

Bobby started to walk away and suddenly stopped in his tracks.

"Oh, may I pick some of those flowers by the mailbox?"

"Why sure, just pick them from the bottom," Mom replied. "Be careful riding your bike."

Bobby pedaled as fast and carefully as he could through the neighborhood. The tall bouquet of daffodils bobbed in his hand as he gripped his handlebars over each sidewalk curb and bump. He parked his bike, marched up the front steps, and rang the doorbell.

Through the peephole, Grandma looked down to see Bobby at the door with both hands behind his back. Bobby could hear her unlocking the door.

Grandma opened the door and smiled, "He's in the bedroom. You can go on back."

Bobby knocked softly on the bedroom door and opened it slowly. He tiptoed into grandfather's bedroom and stood at the foot of the bed. His grandfather looked tired but happy to see him. He grinned.

"Surprise," Bobby said. "Mom said I could pick some for you."

From behind his back, Bobby presented Grandpa with the fresh bunch of flowers.

Grandpa smiled as he rubbed a yellow petal between his fingers and smelled the sweet orange trumpet.

"Oh, daffodils...my favorite! Used to have a slew of' 'em on the farm. They're beautiful... and fancy, too. Plain yellow ones were all we had back then, but boy, how sweet they smelled! Brother Bill and I would set up a roadside stand in front of the house and sell 'em for fifty cents a bunch in a Mason jar. We bought Mother a pretty butterfly pin at the five and dime for Mother's Day with the money we made that spring. She wore that pin to church every Sunday."

He took another whiff of the bouquet and said, "Mmmm, love that smell."

Then Bobby handed him his homemade card. Grandpa held it steady.

His eyes twinkled, "Why, it's beautiful, Bobby."

He rubbed his finger over the crayoned picture of the duck. Grandpa was touched by his grandson's artistic talent and thoughtfulness. His canvasback looked liked the one they had carved together, complete with feather detail and nostrils. Then he opened the card and read the special message.

"Homemade cards are my favorite, Bobby. This one's a keeper. I think we'll be makin' a few more ducks together again. We'll get around all that sawdust, son," he said softly.

Grandpa pulled open his night table drawer and reached inside for his permanent black marker. On top of the table was Bobby's decoy.

"Remember," Grandpa reminded him, "An artist always signs his work."

Bobby gently took the marker from his grandfather's frail but steady hand and signed his name on the bottom of the decoy. Then he signed his name on the canvasback on the front of the card.

Bobby gave Grandpa a tight hug. Grandpa's rough whiskers rubbed against Bobby's tender cheek, but Bobby didn't mind. He was happy now that he knew his Grandpa was going to be getting better. His card cheered him up. Bobby could see that faint gleam in Grandpa's blue eyes.

Esther came in to check on things. She twisted the window blinds open and said, "Gotta have a little light for those daffodils." She winked at Grandpa, "I'll get a Mason jar from under the sink."

After a few days of bed rest, Grandpa was feeling better. Bobby visited him every day and brought in the mail for his grandparents. He even kept the bird feeders filled for Grandma. Bobby and his family remembered that spring when he learned how to carve. For many years, that first canvasback had a special place on the mantle in Bobby's family room. It was followed by many more decoys—mallards, wood ducks, geese, and a swan for Bobby's mother. Grandpa hand chopped the ducks and left the sanding to Bobby. Together, they painted them and made the decoys come to life. He would never forget those tall tales and hunting stories told in Grandpa's basement over Grandma's baked goodies. And someday, he too would pass along his fond memories of his grandparents to his own children, those special memories about how they made each decoy together and shared so many wonderful moments in Grandpa's basement.

Glossary

Audubon: an adjective used to describe a kind of bird calendar or book. John James Audubon was a famous ornithologist who illustrated bird species and painted beautiful bird prints. Naturalists use his species for bird identification and carvers refer to his illustrations when they paint ducks and other birds.

canvasback: a species of diver duck. The hens, or females, are brown and the drakes, or males, have a brown head, a black breast and tail, and a white back like canvas. They were hunted and sold to restaurants. Restaurants wanted them to cook and sell to their customers because canvasbacks were considered one of the best tasting ducks.

decoy: a man-made duck used to lure live ducks close to the hunter. Decoys can be made from reeds, wood, canvas, and cork.

drake: a male duck. The drake has colorful feathers to attract the hen.

duck blind: a concealed or hidden area where hunters hide until the ducks fly over. Blinds can be found in the water and marshes.

hatchet: a small axe similar to a tomahawk. Early carvers used hatchets to hand chop a duck body from a square piece of wood.

hen: a female duck. The hen is usually mostly brown. Hens are brown for camouflage so they can protect their eggs and ducklings.

symmetry: a well balanced arrangement of parts. Carvers needed to make sure their decoys were symmetrical so that they could balance them in the water and remain upright.

wild celery: a type of vegetation that grows in a river or bay. This plant provides oxygen to animals living in the water.

wood duck: a species of duck that arrives in the spring on the Atlantic flyway. It is a colorful bird and makes its home in tree cavities and stumps.

About the Author

Corinne attributes much of her interest in waterfowl and decoys to her Great Uncle Bob Litzenberg, a nationally known decoy carver and furniture maker from Elkton, Maryland. He inspired her to write her first series of children's books, *Flocktales from the Flats*, which teaches about the history of the Chesapeake Bay, decoys, and waterfowl. The illustration of *Grandpa's Basement* on page twelve is taken from an actual photograph by Donna Belinko, of Uncle Bob's basement where he carved many decoys. Decoy carving is an original Americana art form. Decoys were carved for the purpose of hunting waterfowl. Today, many carvers carry on this rich tradition for those who enjoy the sport of duck hunting and for those who collect decoys as a piece of folk art for their home. Corinne feels that decoy carving and its history need to be remembered and preserved by everyone, young and old. She enjoys carving ducks, shorebirds, and songbirds. Corinne has written two other environmental books on the history of the beach, *The Sand Lady: A Cape May Tale* and *The Sand Lady: An Old Ocean City, Maryland Tale*.

About the Illustrator

Inspired by local architecture and rich landscapes, Delaware artist Bari A. Edwards prefers the difficult medium of watercolor because of its translucent quality that defines and enhances her many subjects. Collaborating with Corinne on this third children's book brought back indelible childhood memories of her father's woodshop in the basement of their home. The sound of hammering, the whirl of the lathe, and the smell of sawdust have hopefully been transposed into the illustrations within Grandpa's Basement.

The Carver

A tribute to Robert G. Litzenberg,
Susquehanna Flats Decoy Carver

A hunter sat on his carving stool
And pondered what to carve,
Guess I'll churn out canvasbacks
Or else I'm gonna starve.

He chopped with his hatchet,
Carved mandibles with his blade.
When he had painted his first drake
He thought, "Not bad for the first one made."

He carved a set of fifty
With anchors made of lead,
Every tail was carved straight out
And a shelf made for each head.

The can was called a "North East" duck
And differed from the West.
Across the Flats had upswept tails,
No shelves for heads to rest.

Decoys he made to gun the Flats,
A sport he did enjoy.
His father taught him how to hunt
When he was just a boy.

All admire his fine work
No longer still an amateur.
His talent well surpassed "just ducks"
To Queen Anne furniture.

A craftsman, gentle, kind, and wise,
Qualities beyond a measure.
If you own a duck of his
You know you have a treasure!

Corinne M. Litzenberg